TAKING CARE
OF MOM

BY GINA AND
MERCER MAYER

W9-BSD-991

Westport, Connecticut

Mom was sick. She had a stuffy nose
and a fever.
She had to stay in bed all day. She couldn't
even take us to the playground.

Dad had to go to work, so Grandma
came to pick up my baby brother.
Grandma said my sister and I
should go to her house, too.

But we didn't want to. We wanted to
stay home to take care of Mom.
Grandma said, "All right, but you have
to let your mother rest."

We were really careful not to bother Mom.

We got dressed by ourselves.

We fixed our own breakfast.

I found my favorite game
without asking for help.

I even opened a bag of chips by myself.

We only bothered Mom when it was
really important—like when my sister
spilled the jar of pickles.

We took Mom some juice when we thought she might be thirsty. We only spilled a little bit on her bed.

We fixed Mom a sandwich for lunch.
We didn't know what kind she would want,
so we put a little of everything on it.

We tried to keep the puppy off her bed.
He sure was sneaky though.

We took my mom a hot water bottle to keep her warm. But it leaked a little.

And we brought her another box of tissues. Her
nose was so red.

We even cleaned up a little bit.

I washed the dishes.

My sister picked up some of the toys.

Then we decided to go outside to play.
We put on our own coats and hats.

We told Mom we would be outside
in case she needed us.

We played outside
all afternoon.

When we came back in, Mom looked
like she was feeling a little better.

Mom was better because we took such good care of her. Dad said he thought so, too.

Taking care of Mom was fun.

But I like it a lot better
when she takes care of us.